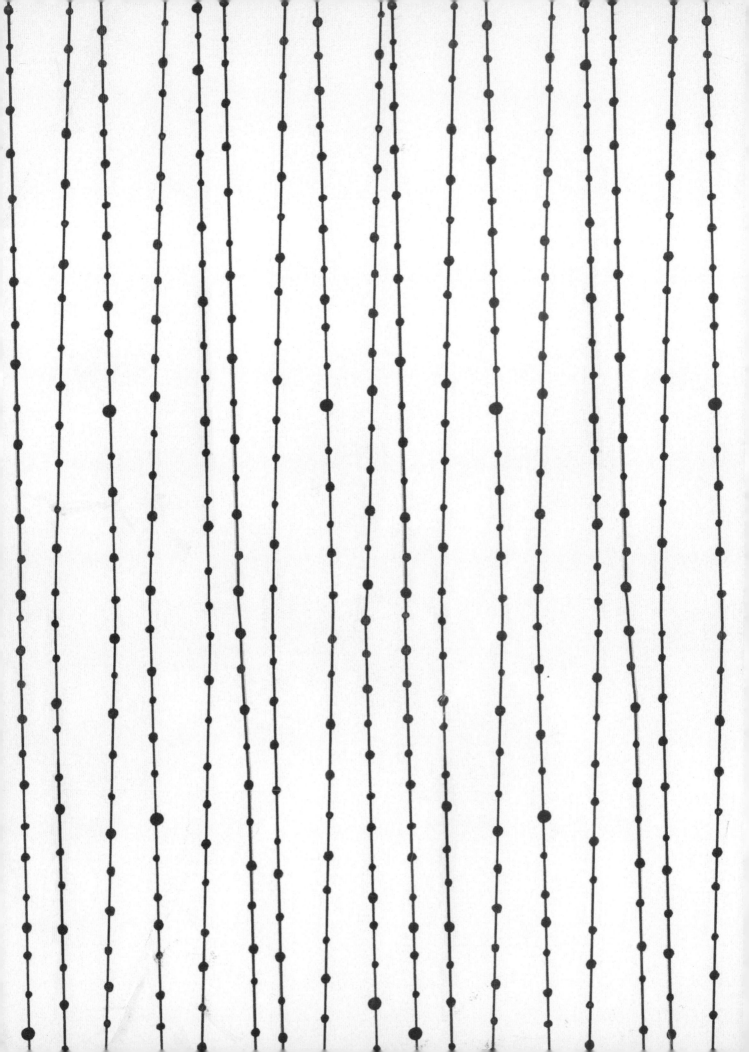

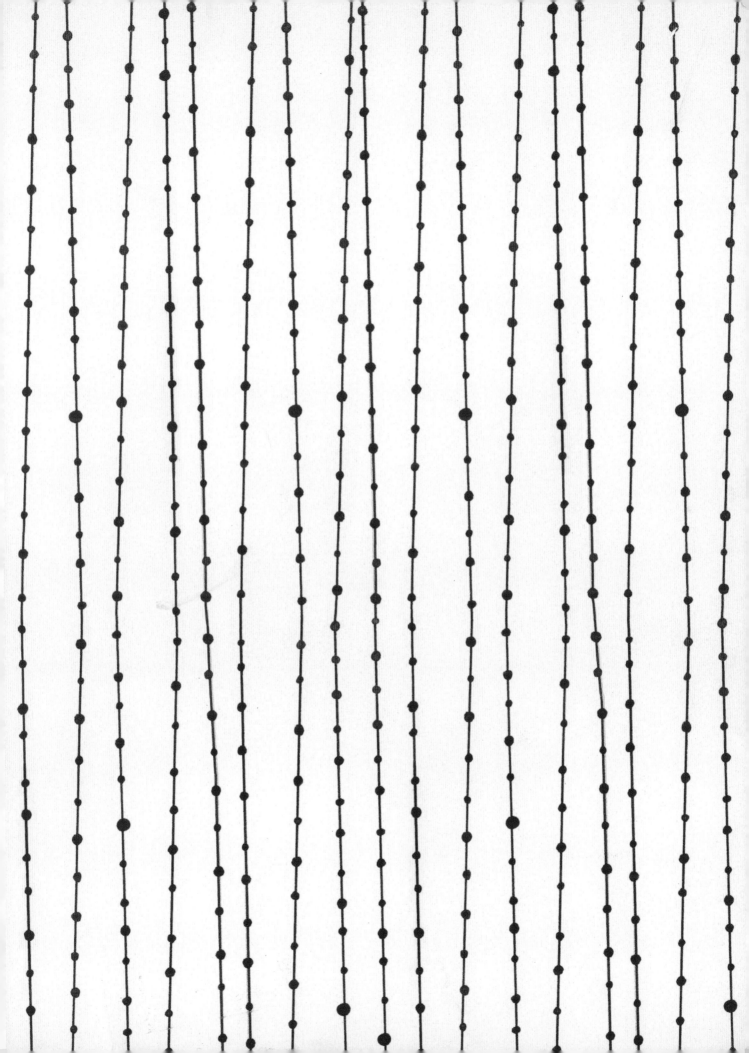

Goldie Locks
Has Chicken Pox

For Paul and Gianna, with love.
And special thanks to Caitlyn Dlouhy.
—E. D. Z.

To Hiromi, Shota, Aiko, Makoto, and Momoko
—H. W.

ALADDIN PAPERBACKS
An imprint of Simon & Schuster Children's Publishing Division
1230 Avenue of the Americas, New York, NY 10020

Text copyright © 2002 by Erin Dealey
Illustrations copyright © 2002 by Hanako Wakiyama

ALADDIN PAPERBACKS and colophon are registered trademarks of Simon & Schuster, Inc.
Also available in an Atheneum Books for Young Readers hardcover edition.

Designed by Edward Miller
The text of this book was set in Imperfect Regular.
Manufactured in China
First Aladdin Paperbacks edition April 2005

2 4 6 8 10 9 7 5 3 1

The Library of Congress has cataloged the hardcover edition as follows:
Dealey, Erin.
Goldie Locks has chicken pox / by Erin Dealey; illustrated by Hanako Wakiyama.–1st ed.
p. cm.
Summary: When Goldie Locks comes down with chicken pox, she is teased by her brother and unable to
visit with Bo Peep, Litle Red Riding Hood, and other friends.
ISBN 0-689-82981-7 (hc.)
[1. Sick–Fiction. 2. Chicken pox–Fiction. 3. Brothers and sisters–Fiction. 4. Characters in literature–Fiction.
5. Stories in rhyme.] I. Title: Goldie Locks has chicken pox. II. Wakiyama, Hanako, ill. III. Title.
PZ8.3.D3415 Go 2002
[E]–dc21 00-045351
ISBN 0-689-87610-6 (pbk.)

To Jared~

Happy Reading!

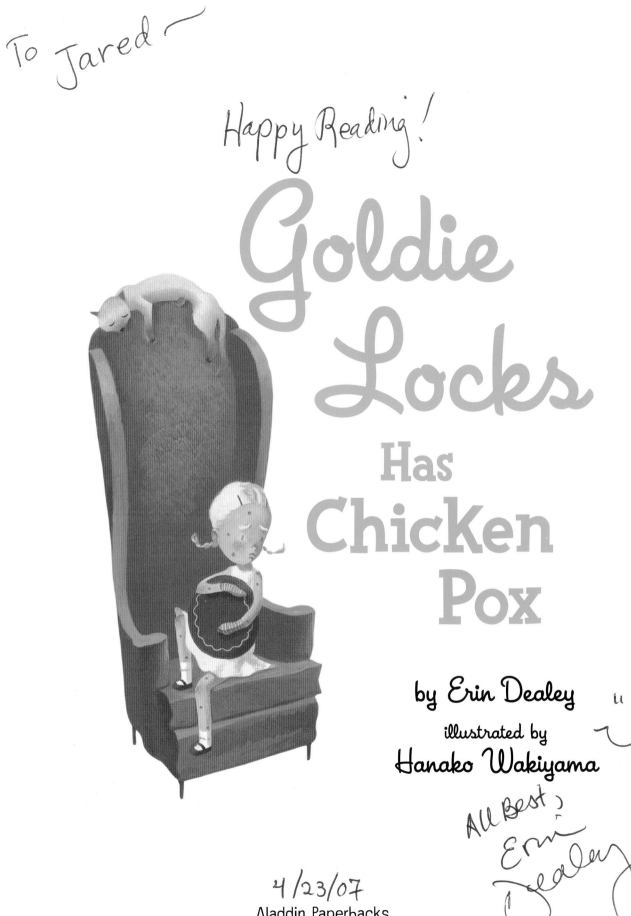

Goldie Locks Has Chicken Pox

by Erin Dealey

illustrated by
Hanako Wakiyama

All Best,
Erin
Dealey

4/23/07

Aladdin Paperbacks
New York London Toronto Sydney

Goldie Locks has chicken pox;
from head to toe were polka dots.

"Where did you get them?" Father said.

But Goldie only shook her head.

Mrs. Locks phoned Mama Bear
(apologizing for the chair),
but Baby Bear did not have spots,
for bears cannot get chicken pox.

"Can chickens get them?"
Brother yelled,
as Henny Penny rang the bell.
"The sky is falling!!!"
Henny squawked.
She had no time for
chicken pox.

"Jack, be nimble! Jack, be quick!
Come and see! My sister's sick!"

But Father told them, "Not today.
When Goldie's better, you can play."

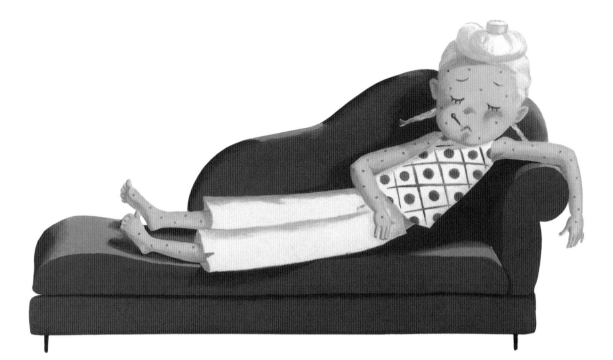

Goldie Locks had chicken pox.

They started out as tiny spots;

then rosy bumps began to form,

and Goldie's temperature was warm.

On her tummy were twenty-four.

On her back, she found twelve more!

All together: thirty-six

small pink dots that itched and itched!

"Please don't scratch them," said her mother.

"Let's connect them!" shouted Brother.

"We might find a teddy bear,
or secret message hidden there!"

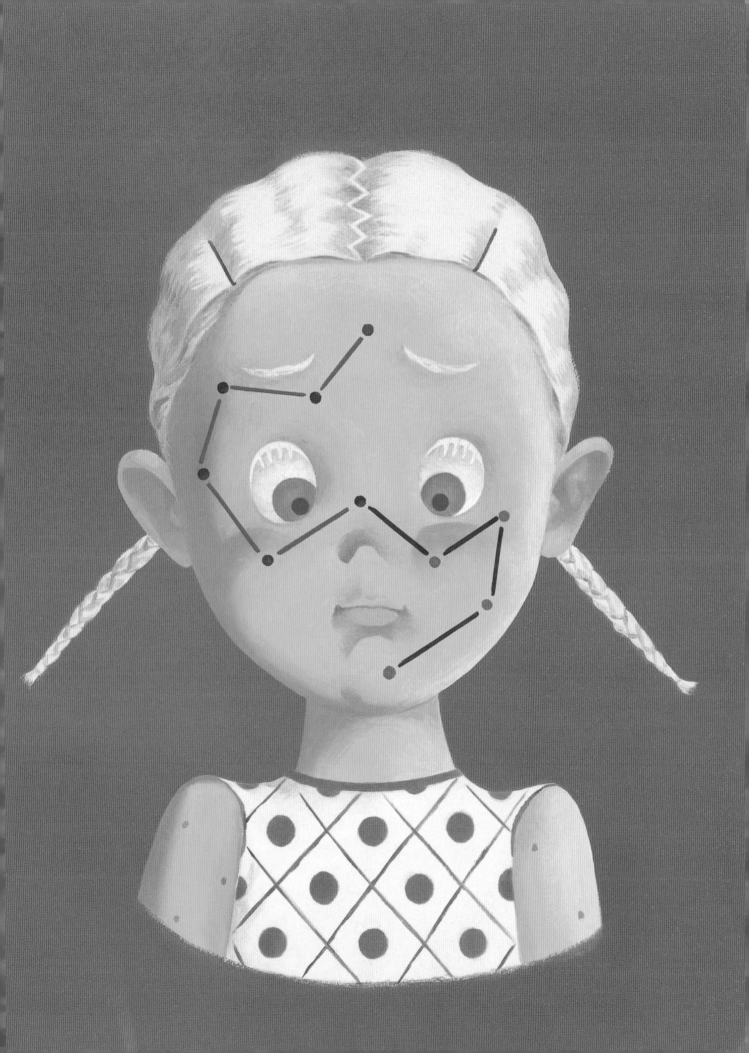

"Leave them be," agreed Bo Peep,
who happened by in search of sheep.
"That's sound advice for chicken pox.
It doesn't work for wayward flocks."

"Goldie Locks has chicken pox,
a type of virus," said the doc.
"Give her sodas, ice cream, too;
a nice cool bath will see her through."

"Yum!" said Brother. "I want some!"

The doctor smiled. "Your time will come . . ."

"No fair!" cried Brother, with a pout.

"She gets it all, and I'm left out!"

Little Red came skipping by,
her basket full of cake and pie.
"Can Goldie come to Gram's with me?
I sure would like the company."

But Goldie Locks had chicken pox;
upon her hands she wore her socks!
"Eek—a monster!!" Brother teased,
"oozing polka-dot disease!!!"

"An alien from outer space!"

Her brother laughed and scratched his face.

"I'm SUPER LOCKS. You can't get me!

My powers are too strong, you see!"

"Make him stop!" cried Goldie Locks.

"I can handle chicken pox!

But how am I supposed to rest

when my brother's such a pest?"

Mother warned him, "That will do!"

And then they saw them, then they knew . . .

Her brother's face showed all the signs,

in rosy polka-dot designs . . .

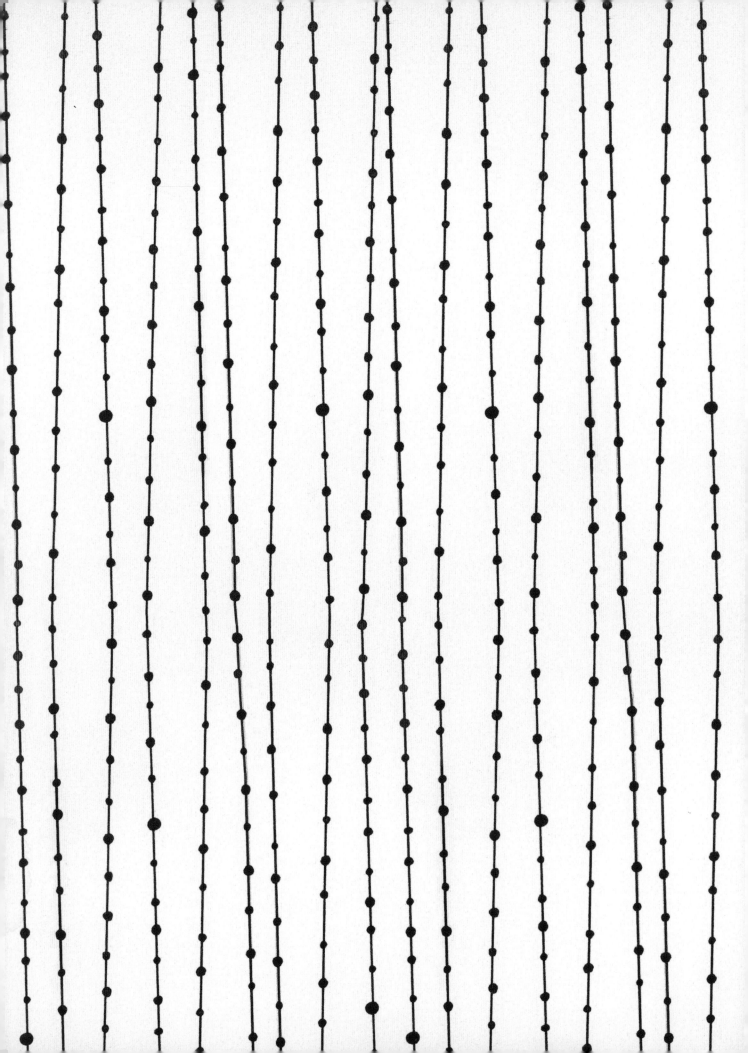

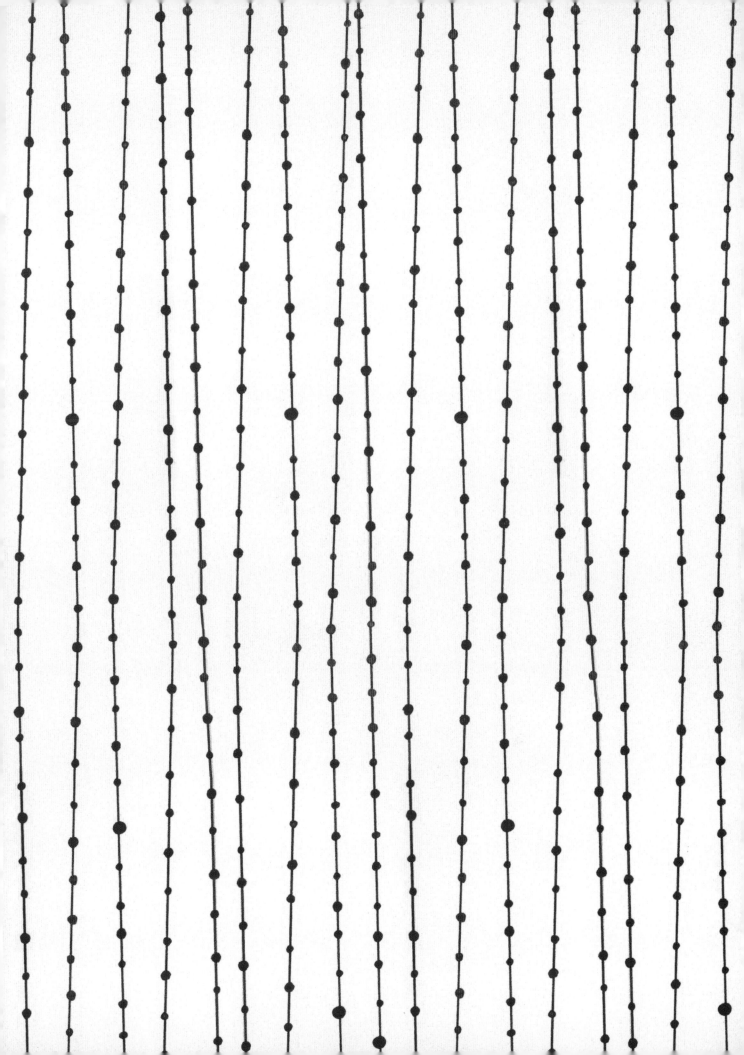